THE SMALLEST TOWN IN THE UNIVERSE

D0795973

SEAN KELLEY McKEEVER
CREATOR/WRITER

ALEXANDRE TEFENKGI
CREATOR/ARTIST

JEAN-FRANCOIS BEAULIEU
COLORIST

ARIANA MAHER
LETTERER

ARIELLE BASICH
ASSOCIATE EDITOR

SEAN MACKIEWICZ
EDITOR

SPECIAL THANKS TO CLIFF CHIANG

Prescott Valley Public Library

OUTPOST ZERO VOLUME 1. FIRST PRINTING. November 2018. Published by Image Comics, Inc. Office of publication: 2701 NW Vaughn St., Ste. 780, Portland, OR 97210. Originally published in single magazine form as OUTPOST ZERO #1-4. OUTPOST ZERO™ (including all prominent characters featured herein), its logo and all character likenesses are trademarks of Skybound, LLC, unless otherwise noted. Image Comics® and its logos are registered trademarks and copyrights of Image Comics, Inc. All rights reserved. No part of this publication may be reproduced or transmitted in any form or by any means (except for short excerpts for review purposes) without the express written permission of Image Comics, Inc. All names, characters, events and locales in this publication are entirely fictional. Any resemblance to actual persons (living or dead), events or places, without satiric intent, is coincidental. Printed in the U.S.A. For information regarding the CPSIA on this printed material call: 203-595-3636 and provide reference RICH# – 818112. ISBN: 978 1 5343 0602 9

volume one

GENSHIP 08
SOMETIMES I DREAM I HIT THE BOTTOM OF THE LAKE, BUT I'M STILL SINKING.
I JUST... KEEP GOING.
GENSHIP ANCESTRY PROJECT
PERSONAL WORLDVIEW STATEMENT
SUBJECT: LINDA
AGE: 17
I WAS THE LAST ONE, AND NOW I'M GONE, TOO, AND I DIDN'T GET TO SEE ANYTHING.
IT JUST ENDS IN THIS MURK. THIS... NOTHING. WORSE THAN NOTHING.
I WISH I COULD BE THERE. WISH I COULD SEE ALL THE INCREDIBLE, ALIEN THINGS.
IF YOU'RE WATCHING THIS...
...I GUESS YOU WERE LUCKY.

NOW DO I GET TO KNOW WHY YOU DRAGGED ME UP HERE?
ALEA?
HI?

THE FOUNDERS HAD TO RECALIBRATE THE GRAVSYNC ENGINE FOR GRAVITY TO WORK IN THE OUTPOST.
YEAH...
TO DO THAT, THEY HAD TO OVERCOMPENSATE. THAT MEANS THERE'S A BIG DIFFERENTIAL AT THE BIOME'S OUTER FRINGES.

AND THAT MEANS WHAT?
IF WE JUMPED RIGHT NOW?
WE'D FLOAT.

NO.
NO WAY.
NO.
YOU DON'T TRUST MY MATH?
YOUR MATH? WE JUMP, WE DIE.
THAT'S JUST--
TEST IT ON A SHOE!
THERE WOULDN'T BE ENOUGH MASS. HARDLY ANY RESISTANCE.
HEY, IT'S NATURAL TO BE SCARED. YOUR BODY DOESN'T WANNA JUMP.
WITH GOOD REASON...
STEVEN.
FORGET YOUR FEARS. COME ON.
ALEA!

NO!

OH.
OH WOW.
HOW...?
HAHA HA!
SEE? YOU SEE THIS?
I KNEW IT. KNEW I WAS--
--WHOA!
WACK

ARE YOU OKAY?!
THINK I BROKE SOMETHING.
ALEA, I DON'T BELIEVE IT. WHEN YOU--
I THOUGHT YOU WERE--
BUT THAT--
THAT WAS INCREDIBLE. YOU WERE RIGHT.
I WAS WRONG.
NORMALIZED GRAVITATION SHOULDN'T HAVE RESUMED THAT HIGH UP.
CHECKED MY MATH OVER AND OVER...
HAS TO BE SOMETHING I MISSED, BUT...
LOOK, JUST...
DON'T EVER DO SOMETHING LIKE THAT AGAIN, OKAY?
OKAY?
OKAY?

ZZZZ
FSSSSS
WHAT A SUNRISE.

I HAVEN'T SEEN ONE OF THESE IN FOREVER.
YOU HAVEN'T BEEN UP THIS EARLY IN FOREVER.
I'M SURE THAT BREAK DIDN'T HELP YOU SLEEP ANY.
I'D TELL YOU TO STOP FALLING, BUT YOU INHERITED MY COORDINATION.

YOU DIDN'T HAVE TO SEE US OFF, ALEA.
I'VE STILL GOT A LOT TO LEARN FOR WHEN I JOIN DISCOVERY TEAM.
YOU'LL BE INTERNING IN A FEW WEEKS. NO NEED TO RUSH.

YOU'RE GONNA FIND SOMETHING THIS TIME, LIFE. I KNOW IT.
I WANNA BE OUT THERE IN THE FROST, DAD--FINDING IT WITH YOU GUYS.
ONE STEP AT A TIME. YOU HAVEN'T EVEN MADE YOUR OWN SUIT YET.

NOW--WHO'S IN CHARGE WHILE I'M GONE?
ME.
AND WHO ELSE?
NO ONE.
GOT THAT RIGHT.

JANN.
DENIS.
AIRLOCK'S OPEN.
LET'S MOVE IT.
THE CHIEF HAS SPOKEN...

CAST COMES OFF TONIGHT.
YEAH?
SOON AS THAT HAPPENS, WHAT ARE YOU ***NOT*** GOING TO DO?
JUMP.
THANK YOU.

NOT UNTIL I FIGURE OUT WHERE I WENT WRONG.
WILL YOU LET ME ASSUME THAT'S A JOKE?
PLEASE?

HOPE WE'RE INTERRUPTING SOMETHING.
YEAH, WAY TO GO, ***MITCHELL.*** WE WERE ABOUT TO BE ALL KISSY ON EACH OTHER WITH OUR MOUTHS.

I HAVEN'T SEEN ***MADDIE*** IN A WHILE. IS SHE...?
EVIL TWIN'S OFF BEING EVIL.
IF YOU'RE GOOD AT SOMETHING, DO IT, I SAY.

HEY, BE SURE TO CONGRATULATE ***LYSS.*** TODAY SHE GETS TOLD ***WHAT TO DO*** FOR THE REST OF HER LIFE.
YOUR ***APTITUDE*** ASSIGNMENT? WHY DIDN'T YOU SAY? WANT ME TO GO?
IT'S NOT A BIG DEAL. SERIOUSLY.

WHATEVER THEY DECIDE, I'LL BE FINE.
OH!
AND MY ***SINGULARITY*** IS ALMOST HERE!
TWENTY DAYS.

YOUR WHAT? SINGULARITY? WHY, THIS IS THE FIRST I'M HEARING OF IT IN THE LAST FIVE MINUTES.
MITCHELL--

UH.
SAM. HEY. WHAT'S UP?
DID YOU--? DO YOU STILL WANT TO...?
YEAH! ABSOLUTELY. LET'S GRAB A TABLE.

WHAT IS STEVEN DOING WITH THAT WASTE OF FLESH?
I KEEP TRYING TO TELL HIM--THE PROBLEM WITH BEING NICE TO EVERYBODY IS YOU HAVE TO BE NICE TO EVERYBODY.
I BARELY KNOW HIM.
HE'S ALREADY INTERNING PART-TIME WITH SECURITY TEAM.

THE CHIEF PULLED SOME STRINGS. NOW HE'S FOLLOWING IN HIS FOSTER MOMMY'S FOOTSTEPS.

SOMEDAY OUR LIVES'LL BE IN THE HANDS OF THAT SPINELESS FREAK.
AND WE'LL ALL DIE.

...SO DOES THE LESSON MEAN, EVEN PUTTING ASIDE ENERGY AND WASTE ISSUES, IF THE BIOME SEPARATED FROM THE STEM WE'D BE STRUCTURALLY COMPROMISED, OR...?
SAM? EVERYTHING OKAY?

DO YOU EVER THINK ABOUT WHAT'S OUT THERE?
LIKE... OUT IN THE FROST?
NO. IN THE UNIVERSE.

ALL THE GENSHIPS THAT REACHED THEIR DESTINATIONS AND BUILT NEW HOMES.
THE PEOPLE OUR ANCESTORS LEFT BEHIND.
WHAT KIND OF LIVES DO THEY HAVE? WHAT ARE THEY DOING? DO THEY FEEL THE WAY...?
ARE THEY WHERE THEY BELONG?

WOW. I DON'T-- I MEAN, I DON'T KNOW. I GUESS I DON'T THINK ABOUT IT.
I KNOW THEY'RE TESTING THAT RADIO TO GET SIGNALS FROM SPACE, BUT THIS IS OUR UNIVERSE, YOU KNOW?
THE OUTPOST.

ANYTHING OUTSIDE THESE WALLS...
DOES IT EVEN REALLY MATTER?

WE'VE GOT NINETY-SEVEN HOURS OF PEAK DAY LEFT. HOW'S IT GOING?
DRILL'S FUSSY AGAIN. FABRICATION TEAM HAS TO COME THROUGH ON THAT NEW ACTUATOR.
THAT'S FIFTH ON OUR LIST WITH THEM.
YEAH.
AND THE FIRST WON'T BE READY FOR TWELVE WEEKS.
YEAH...
DENIS... DID ALEA SEEM WEIRD TO YOU?
SHE'S FOURTEEN. SO, YES.
FOURTEEN. AND SOON A RESPONSIBLE WORKER. A LIVING, BREATHING TEDIUM--JUST LIKE US.
RIIIGHT.
I FEEL GOOD ABOUT THIS SPOT.
WE'LL FIND SOMETHING. SOLID GROUND, SIGNS OF LIFE...
THINK SO, JANN?
NO.
BUT WHAT'S THE ALTERNATIVE?

WHAT WAS THAT WITH YOU TWO AT LUNCH?
AREN'T YOU NOSY?
HEY. AVOIDING THE QUESTION'LL JUST MAKE ME MORE CURIOUS. AND YOU KNOW WHAT THAT MEANS.
YEAH. YOU'LL JUST GET MORE STUBBORN.
MORE PERSISTENT.
SAM'S HELPING ME WITH ENGINEERING STUFF. HE'S A SMART GUY.
APTITUDE PREP AT LUNCH? SO YOU REALLY ARE ALL ABOUT ENGINEERING TEAM NOW.
WE NEED ENGINEERS.
NOT JUST TO MAINTAIN THE OUTPOST, BUT TO BUILD STRONGER FOUNDATIONS.
BESIDES, YOU KNOW WHAT IT WOULD DO TO MY DAD IF I DIDN'T FOLLOW HIS PATH.
I DO...
...THAT WEIRD VEIN IN HIS FOREHEAD WOULD FINALLY POP.
IT WOULD. IT ABSOLUTELY WOULD...
HEY...
WHY ARE YOU HERE?

ASSUMING YOU DON'T MEAN EXISTENTIALLY...
LYSS SAYS SHE DOESN'T CARE. MAYBE THAT'S TRUE, BUT SOME THINGS...WE DON'T KNOW WHAT THEY'LL DO TO US 'TIL THEY HAPPEN.

BUT YOU WERE GOING TO WATCH THEM TEST THE RADIO. YOU WERE ALL EXCITED.
IF IT WORKS, WE'LL HEAR ABOUT IT. IT'S NOT LIKE WE'D GET AN IMMEDIATE SIGNAL--
THERE SHE IS.

WELL?
"NO PARTICULAR APTITUDE". THEY'RE PUTTING ME WHERE THEY NEED STAFF.
I'LL BE ON SERVICES TEAM.

YOU MEAN SHIT TEAM!
DON'T--
I TOLD YOU TO STUDY WITH YOUR MOTHER FOR MEDICAL TEAM! NOW MY GIRL WILL BE UP TO HER EYEBALLS IN HUMAN EXCREMENT, WORKING WITH CRIMINALS!
I'LL APPEAL--

DAD, IT'S FINE.
REALLY, I DON'T MIND.
SOMEONE HAS TO DO IT. WHY FORCE MYSELF TO BE SOMETHING I'M NOT?

GUESS SHE'S GONNA BE OKAY.
I... GUESS?

ANCIENT, GLITCHY, DUMBHEADED--
COME ON, JUNKBOX! SHOW ME THE RIGHT--

THE RIGHT...

DENIS?
YOU CAN DO IT, DRILL...HOLD OUT A LITTLE LONGER...
AMBIENT ANALYSIS: 98.7% COMPLETE

DENIS.
MM? WHAT HAVE YOU GOT, JANN?

THIS.

AMBIENT ANALYSIS:
SAMPLE FOUND. COMPILI

BZZZ

IT'LL FEEL STIFF FOR A COUPLE DAYS, BUT--
I'M SURE LYSS'LL BE OKAY.
WHAT?
OH.
YES.

HER *FATHER* WAS SO UPSET.
BUT NOT YOU.
MY SWEET GIRL GETS IT-- WE ALL HAVE TO PLAY OUR PART OR THERE'S NO OUTPOST. AND ANYWAY...

...SHE HAS FRIENDS LIKE YOU AND STEVEN AT HER SIDE.

HEY. THEY DIDN'T EUTHANIZE YOU.
BETTER LUCK NEXT TIME.

WHY ARE YOU HERE? WHAT'S GOING ON?
ASSUMING YOU DON'T MEAN EXISTENTIALLY...?

DID YOU HEAR ABOUT THE RADIO?
YEAH. REPRO TEAM DIDN'T GET THE CIRCUITRY RIGHT. MORE ADVANCED THAN THEY THOUGHT.
HUMANS INVENTED THIS STUFF. YOU'D THINK WE COULD FIGURE IT OUT AGAIN, BUT--
HEY!
IS THIS WHERE YOU WERE TAKING US?
WE CAME HERE EVERY DAY. YOU AND MITCHELL, ME AND MADDIE.
I'VE BEEN THINKING ABOUT MADDIE AND MITCHELL'S MOM. HOW SHE WORKED THE FARMS.
MITCHELL SAYS THAT WAS ALL SHE EVER WANTED TO DO HER WHOLE LIFE.
PROVIDING FOR OTHERS. HANDS IN THE DIRT. SHE KNEW IN HER HEART SHE WANTED THAT LIFE. AND THEN--
SHE WOUND UP HATING IT 'TIL THE DAY SHE DIED. MADDIE TOLD ME ONCE.
WHAT'S THIS MEAN? YOU'RE HAVING SECOND THOUGHTS ABOUT ENGINEERING TEAM?
THIS ISN'T ABOUT ME.

ME? I'LL NEVER HATE DISCOVERY TEAM.
YOU DON'T KNOW THAT FOR SURE.
WHAT'S YOUR--? WHAT ARE YOU SAYING?
YOUR FOLKS ARE ALL THAT'S LEFT OF DISCOVERY TEAM.
EVERYONE ELSE DIED.
HORRIBLY, OUT IN THAT WASTELAND, AND FOR WHAT?
THAT COULD'VE BEEN YOU THE OTHER NIGHT.
WHAT, THE LEAP? IT WAS A WEIRD LITTLE ANOMALY.
I'M WORKING OUT WHAT WENT WRONG, SO DON'T--
I'M SAYING, WHAT YOUR PARENTS DO IS TOO DANGEROUS.
STEVEN--THE WALLS COULD BREAK. OR THE DOME.
CROPS COULD FAIL. WE COULD OVER-POPULATE.
THE ENERGY MATRIX COULD SPUTTER OUT.
WE'RE AT RISK ALL THE TIME. ALL OF US. THAT'S DANGEROUS.
OUR ANCESTORS CRASH-LANDED ON A BALL OF ICE.
THERE'S A CHANCE WE CAN FIND A WAY TO LIVE HERE.
REALLY LIVE.
THRIVE.
THE GRAVITY OUT THERE'S NOT TOO BAD.
BUT--
TEMPERATURE ASIDE, THE AIR'S BREATHABLE. THERE'S TONS OF USABLE WATER. WE CAN ADAPT TO THE LONG DAY CYCLES...

I HAVE TO BE A PART OF MAKING THAT HAPPEN.
IT'S IN MY BONES.

LISTEN TO YOU.
FOR ALL WE KNOW, WE'RE THE LAST HUMAN BEINGS-- AND WE'RE NOT DOING SO GREAT.
WE'RE ***CRAWLING,*** AND ***YOU*** WANT TO ***RUN.***

WE HAVEN'T DROPPED UNDER ONE PERCENT OF PEAK POPULATION FOR GENERATIONS.
THAT'S BECAUSE EVERYTHING WE DO, WE ***HAVE*** TO DO TO STAY ALIVE.

WHAT WE ***DON'T*** HAVE TO DO IS JEOPARDIZE EVERY LAST ONE OF US BECAUSE WE KEEP OPENING A DOOR TO GO OUTSIDE INTO ***THE FROST.***

IT'S AN ***AIRLOCK.*** THERE'S NO DANGER.
AND THE GRAVSYNC DIFFERENTIAL IS TOTALLY SAFE, RIGHT?
I ***TOLD*** YOU--

I'M SORRY, ALEA, I AM.
BUT YOU AND YOUR PARENTS? YOU'RE CHASING A FANTASY.

FORGET ABOUT THRIVING.
WE NEED TO ***SURVIVE.***

I FORGOT THE DRILL. THE ANALYSIS--
DENIS-- SCREW THE ANALYSIS.
I NEED THE CHIEF.
KAREN, GET ME KAREN.
YOU'RE BACK EARLY. WE'RE NOT READY TO DECONTAMINATE--
STOP TALKING AND LISTEN.
GET THE COUNCIL TOGETHER. PLANNING TEAM, TOO. THEY NEED TO HAVE A LOOK AT WHAT WE--
AND START THE ALARMS.
AND START THE ALARMS.
WHAT IS IT?
IF WE'RE RIGHT, IT'S TEN YEARS AGO.
BUT WORSE.

AS OF HALF AN HOUR AGO, ***IMMINENT EVENT PROTOCOLS*** ARE IN EFFECT.
A CELL IS APPROACHING.
IT WAS FIRST DETECTED EARLY THIS MORNING FROM AN EXPEDITION IN THE FROST.
ATMOSPHERIC INTERFERENCE PREVENTED ***DISCOVERY TEAM*** FROM INFORMING US REMOTELY.
WE ONLY ***RECENTLY*** LEARNED OF THE CELL'S EXISTENCE.
THE FRONT IS EXPECTED TO REACH THE OUTPOST IN APPROXIMATELY FOUR HOURS.
THAT LEAVES US THREE AND A HALF TO ***PREPARE.***
UNLESS YOU ARE ON PREPARATION DETAIL, YOU ARE TO JOIN YOUR FAMILIES ***IMMEDIATELY*** FOLLOWING THIS ASSEMBLY. NO EXCEPTIONS.

WE DON'T HAVE A FULL PICTURE OF ITS INTENSITY YET, BUT WE COMPARED WHAT WE KNOW TO HISTORICAL DATA.
FROM ALL INDICATIONS, THE CELL IS LARGER THAN THE ONE THAT HIT TEN YEARS AGO...

...WHEN IT BREACHED THE DOME AND TOOK THE EASTERN REGION, ALONG WITH HUNDREDS OF LIVES.
HEY. SAM.

ISN'T THAT THE STORM THAT PUT YOUR FOLKS ON ICE?

NOW, MOST OF YOU ARE OLD ENOUGH TO REMEMBER--
PLEASE, EVERYONE, STAY SEATED! DON'T PANIC.

MITCHELL...
WORTH IT.

SAM...
YOU CAN'T LET HIM GET UNDER YOUR SKIN.
IT WASN'T WHAT HE SAID. I'VE HEARD WORSE.
I JUST...

I FELT EXPOSED.

EVERYONE LOOKED AT ME, AND THEY COULD... THEY COULD ALL ***SEE*** ME.
UH...? I'M NOT SURE I...

JUST A SECOND, OKAY? I HAVE TO--
JUST WAIT.

ALEA...
I HAVE TO SEE IF I'M NEEDED. BE SAFE.

I SHOULD NEVER HAVE SAID--
IT WAS HURTFUL AND--
IS THIS BECAUSE OF THE CELL? BECAUSE WE MIGHT ALL--
NO. NO, THAT'S NOT--

SO THEN YOU DIDN'T MEAN IT, THAT DISCOVERY TEAM IS SOME CRAZY FANTASY?
OR DID YOU?

STEVEN!

YOUR INTERNSHIP STARTS NOW.
DAD?
BUT I HAVEN'T BEEN TRAINED FOR--

THERE'S NO TRAINING LIKE DOING.
LET'S GO!
BE SAFE.

YOU, TOO.

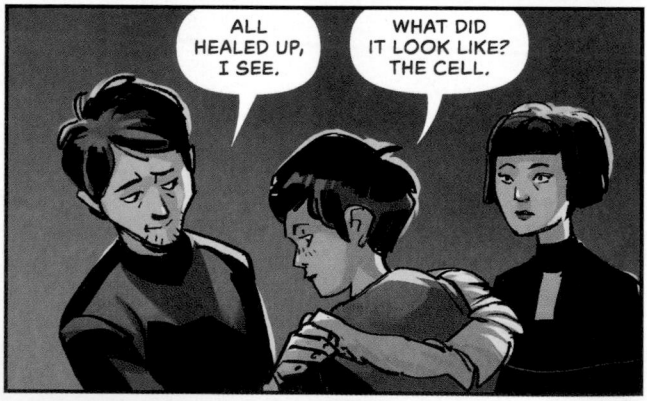
ALL HEALED UP, I SEE.
WHAT DID IT LOOK LIKE? THE CELL.

WE DIDN'T ACTUALLY SEE IT. JUST RADAR.
BUT IT'S AS BIG AS THEY'RE SAYING. WE HAVE TO MAKE SURE WE'RE LOCKED DOWN.

YOUR SISTER'S WORKING ON HER ROOM. WE SHOULD BE GETTING TO IT, TOO.
THAT'S IT? WE DON'T HAVE ANY, LIKE, OFFICIAL DUTIES?
WE'RE ON CALL FOR OUR EXPERTISE, BUT...
WHAT, NOW DISCOVERY TEAM ISN'T ESSENTIAL TO OUR SURVIVAL?
WHAT DO YOU MEAN? OF COURSE WE'RE ESSENTIAL.
THERE ARE PEOPLE--THEY DON'T THINK SO. THEY SAY WE SHOULD BE MORE PRACTICAL.
YES, BUT THOSE PEOPLE CAN'T THINK PAST TODAY. THEY'RE MYOPIC. OR SCARED. OR BOTH.
THEY NEED DISCOVERY TEAM, END OF STORY.
NOW LET'S GET TO WORK.
IF WE'RE NOT READY, WE COULD LOSE EVERYTHING.

FSSSS
FSSSS
UH...
SPUT
SPUT
SPUT
BLAST
AAAH!
GOT YA!
TOLD YOU, WATCH FOR AIR POCKETS IN THE LINE!
SORRY.
SORRY NOTHING.
YOU DON'T FOCUS, YOU FALL. YOU FALL...
...YOU DIE.
DON'T BE SO SURE...

...I DON'T KNOW HOW OR WHY, BUT THIS IS WHAT I AM NOW.
I CAN'T GO BACK.
I WANT TO TELL SOMEONE. I WISH I COULD. BUT THE BURDEN OF KNOWING WHAT I'M CAPABLE OF...
...I CAN'T PUT THAT ON ANYONE. HOW COULD I DO THAT TO THEM?
IT'D BE EASIER IF I COULD DISAPPEAR. BE FORGOTTEN, LIKE AN ORCHID UNDER THE SNOW.
LIKE A STONE DROPPED INTO A LAKE.
I EVEN DREAM ABOUT IT.
SOMETIMES I DREAM I HIT THE BOTTOM OF THE LAKE, BUT--
SAM?

SAM.
YEAH?
WHAT ARE YOU DOING?
NOTHING.
I SAW YOU LEFT THE BRIEFING--
IT'S FINE.
REALLY.
OKAY.
THE DEAN WAS WORRIED, IS ALL.
I CAN'T STAY. I WON'T BE HOME UNTIL AFTER.
I KNOW.
I NEED YOU TO SECURE THE DOORS AND WINDOWS.
OKAY.
DON'T GO ANYWHERE.
YOU'LL BE OKAY.
OKAY.

WHAT IS IT, KID?

I WANNA SEE THE REAL SKY. WHAT'S COMING.
THIS IS FAKE. IT'S WRONG.
YEP.

MOST PEOPLE NEED A VEIL TO PROTECT THEM FROM REALITY, ALEA.

BUT NOT US.

I WISH I COULD BE THERE. WISH I COULD SEE ALL THE INCREDIBLE, ALIEN THINGS.
IF YOU'RE WATCHING THIS...
...I GUESS YOU WERE LUCKY.

I MADE A NOTE.
NOT TO EXPLAIN WHY I'M DOING THIS.
THE WAY THINGS ARE NOW, THE WAY THEY'RE ABOUT TO GET, IT'LL BE OBVIOUS.

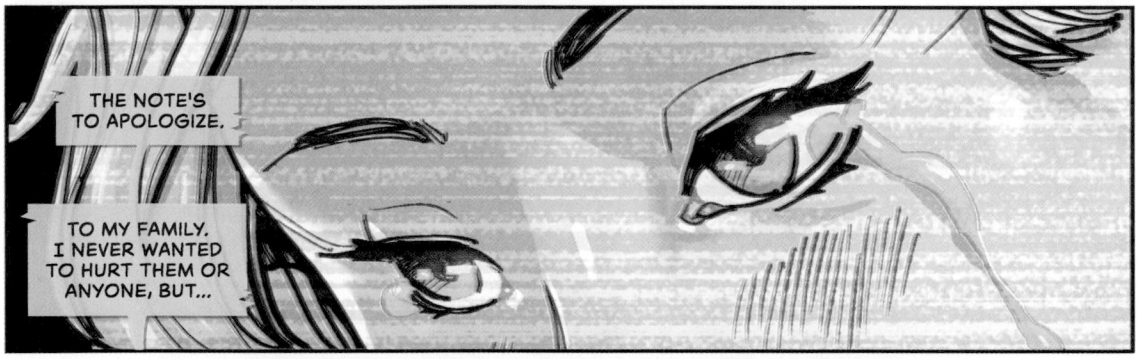
THE NOTE'S TO APOLOGIZE.
TO MY FAMILY. I NEVER WANTED TO HURT THEM OR ANYONE, BUT...

I KNOW THEY'LL SAY I WAS WEAK. SELFISH. WASN'T MYSELF.
SOON ENOUGH, I WON'T HAVE TO CARE WHAT THEY THINK. EVER.

JUST ONE FAVOR BEFORE I GO, OKAY?

THIS NEW WORLD YOU GET TO MAKE-- MORE THAN ANYTHING, I HOPE YOU CH-CH-
CH-
CH-
CH-
CH-
CH-
CH-

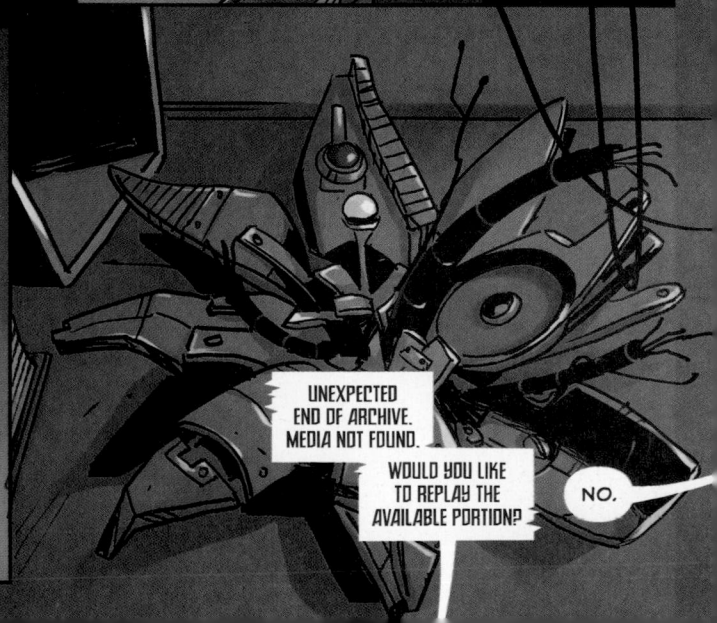
UNEXPECTED END OF ARCHIVE. MEDIA NOT FOUND.
WOULD YOU LIKE TO REPLAY THE AVAILABLE PORTION?
NO.

ELLA? WHAT IS IT?
I KNOW I'M NOT SUPPOSED TO GO INTO ALEA'S ROOM, BUT THERE WAS A NOISE.
LOOK WHAT THAT DUMMY DID.
ALEA?!
ALEA!
WHAT'S HAPPENING?!
THEY TURNED OFF THE SKY.
IT'S ALMOST TIME.

HEY THERE. WAS JUST ABOUT TO SEAL THE--
WAIT, WHAT'S WRONG?

WHY AREN'T YOU HOME? EVERYTHING OKAY?
STEVEN.
I NEED TO SEE HIM.

IT'S ALMOST TIME. YOU SHOULD BE TUCKED AWAY WITH YOUR FAMILY.
I CAN STAY HERE UNTIL IT PASSES.
IT'S FINE. PLEASE.

STEVEN!
HE ISN'T HERE!
GO TO HIS ROOM AND GET HIM, TARIN!
I CAN'T! HE LEFT!

LEFT?! LEFT WHERE?!

ZZZIP
"SOON ENOUGH...
"I WON'T HAVE TO CARE..."

NO SIGNS OF SABOTAGE HERE, CHIEF. WANT US TO KEEP AT IT?
NO. YOU GET SAFE.

CHIEF--
DID THEY FOAM ALL THE SEAMS? DO WE KNOW?
ABOUT NINETY PERCENT, BUT, CHIEF--

ONLY NINETY? GOT TO BE KIDDING...
KAREN. IT'S YOUR BOY--IT'S SAM.
OKAY. PUT HIM ON SPEAKER.
NO, HE DIDN'T CALL...

HE'S...
HE'S IN THE AIRLOCK.

S-STEVEN...

WH-
WHAT ARE
YOU WAITING
F-FOR...
GET
IT OVER
WITH!!

AMBIENT
ANALYSIS
SAMPLE
BIO-COMPLEXITY
VALUE:

HE WAS GOING TO MAKE A FINE ENGINEER.
WOULD HAVE BEEN A GOOD DAD. A GREAT DAD.
DECENT TO EVERYONE.
PATIENT.
I THOUGHT--
I THOUGHT I RAISED HIM TO BE STRONGER...

HOW DID HE EVEN GET TO THE FROST? THE AIRLOCK'S CODED.
DOESN'T MAKE SENSE.
REMEMBER WHEN STEVEN BROKE HIS JAW?

HE COULD ONLY EAT LIQUIDS. DRINK THEM, WHATEVER.
HE'D GARGLE EVERYTHING JUST TO GET ME TO LAUGH.
THAT ONE TIME HIS LUNCH ALMOST CHOKED HIM TO DEATH.

LYSS...
WHAT'S THAT GOT TO DO WITH HIM GETTING OUTSIDE?
IT'S JUST A FUN MEMORY.

UHM, HELLO.
I'M, UH, I'M SORRY YOUR SON'S GONE.

YOU'RE THE CHIEF'S... HER BOY.
SAM.
YOU UNDERSTAND. THERE'S TOO MUCH LOSS, ISN'T THERE?
FAR TOO MUCH.

DID YOU KNOW MY STEVEN?
I DID. HE WAS GOOD TO ME.

WE ALL FEEL THE PULL, BUT WE CONTAIN IT.
AN EPIDEMIC OF SELFISHNESS IS SPREADING THROUGH OUR YOUTH, DEAN.

THIS ONE DIDN'T EVEN HAVE THE DECENCY TO LET US COMPOST HIS REMAINS.
MITCHELL, WHERE'S MADDIE? DON'T TELL ME SHE DIDN'T EVEN SHOW...

HEY, LOOK, YOU KNOW STEVEN COULDN'T HAVE DONE WHAT THEY'RE SAYING. WE BOTH DO.
SOMEONE'S NOT TELLING US SOMETHING, AND WE--

MITCHELL.
MITCHELL, I'M NOT KIDDING.

STEVEN WAS--
HE WAS A COWARD.

I THOUGHT HE WAS STRONG--BUT HE WAS A COWARD LIKE ALL THE OTHERS!
KEEP YOUR VOICE--
HE GAVE UP ON EVERYONE AND KILLED HIMSELF!
THAT'S ALL!
COWARD!

GOT SOME GOOD NEWS.
DOES IT MAKE SENSE TO YOU, DAD?
HOW STEVEN COULD'VE GOTTEN INTO THE AIRLOCK?
IF SOMEONE WANTS SOMETHING BAD ENOUGH, THEY CAN GET AWFULLY CREATIVE.
BUT HE DIDN'T WANT THIS.
I WOULD'VE KNOWN.
YOU CAN'T GET STUCK IN YOUR OWN HEAD ABOUT IT, ALEA. THAT ISN'T HOW INSIGHT WORKS.
SO, BACK TO THAT GOOD NEWS...
WE'RE CLEARED FOR YOU TO START YOUR INTERNSHIP AHEAD OF SCHEDULE.

SERIOUS?
WITH ALL THAT ICE THE CELL DUMPED OVER US, WE DON'T KNOW WHEN WE'LL GET BACK OUT, BUT THAT DOESN'T MEAN THERE'S NOTHING TO DO.
YOUR MOM AND I HAVE STARTED TO ASSIST PLANNING TEAM. WE FIGURE YOU CAN, TOO.

PLANNING TEAM.
SO...
NOT DISCOVERY TEAM.

THEY'RE A SMART BUNCH OF PEOPLE DOING IMPORTANT WORK. YOU'LL LEARN A LOT--
Y'KNOW WHAT, FORGET THE INTERNSHIP. I NEED TO KNOW WHAT HAPPENED TO STEVEN!

HEY.
HEY, I KNOW...
BUT THERE'S ONLY ONE WAY TO KNOW THE TRUTH ABOUT WHAT HE DID...

...AND HE'S NOT AROUND TO ASK ANYMORE.

THOUGHT I HAD IT WORKED OUT. I WAS DONE.
THERE WAS JUST... NOTHING ELSE FOR ME.
THEN YOU SHOW UP, YOU... YOU SAY THOSE *WORDS?*
STEVEN...
AND THEN YOU GO ***OUTSIDE*** INSTEAD OF ME, AND...
...
AND I DON'T KNOW WHAT NOW.

SSSRRR

HI.
A LITTLE WORSE FOR WEAR, HUH?
SSSRRR

--JUST WANTED TO SAY--
--I NEED TO SAY--
--THE THING YOU NEED TO REALIZE, STEVEN--

THERE YOU GO...

THAT DIDN'T WORK, DID IT? NOW YOU'RE GOING IN CIRCLES...

DON'T WORRY, I'LL FIX--

--YOU--

UHHN!
GET AWAY!
YOU DON'T GET TO SIT HERE AND TALK TO HIM, YOU WASTE OF FLESH, YOU HAVE NO RIGHT.
YOU DIDN'T KNOW HIM, YOU DIDN'T KNOW!
I...
I KNEW HIM WELL ENOUGH TO KNOW HE WASN'T A COWARD.
GET UP.

NRAAAGH!
THOK
I DON'T WANT TO SEE YOU HERE AGAIN.

SOMETHING'S BROKEN. DO YOU SEE IT?
ROLLING BROWNOUTS FROM THE STORM CELL MADE IT WORSE, BUT THE AUDIT SHOWS THE ENERGY DISCREPANCY HAS ALWAYS BEEN THERE.
ALEA? ARE YOU FOLLOWING THIS?
THE NUMBERS ON ONE LIST AREN'T THE SAME AS THE ONES ON THE OTHER LIST. GOT IT, KANAAN.
I KNOW. THIS STUFF IS... ABSTRACT.
WE'RE USUALLY CONCERNED WITH JUICIER TOPICS AT PLANNING TEAM. POPULATION, CONSUMPTION, WORK-LIFE BALANCE OPTIMIZATION.
BUT OUR FOCUS NOW IS THE IMMEDIATE THREAT OF SIX STORIES OF ICE WEIGHING DOWN ON US.
ANALYZING DATA MIGHT NOT BE AS EXCITING AS A DISCOVERY TEAM EXPEDITION, BUT SO FAR NO ONE'S DIED.
BECAUSE OF OUR EMERGENCY PROTOCOLS, I MEANT. I DIDN'T--
I MEAN...

--COULD VENT STEAM IF PRESSURE ZONES EMERGE, BUT THAT'S JUST TEMPORARY.
IF WE SENT A HIGH ENOUGH CURRENT THROUGH THE DOME, THE HEAT WOULD REACH THE ICE.
AND FRY THE DISPLAY MATRIX ALONG THE WAY. WE'D LOSE OUR SKY, DENIS.
THE PSYCHOLOGICAL RAMIFICATIONS--
BETTER TO BE ALIVE, OF COURSE, BUT LET'S FIND A LESS ADVERSE SOLUTION. AFTER ALL...

...WE DON'T WANT TO INCREASE THE RISK OF SELF-EXPIRATION IF WE CAN HELP IT.

WHERE ARE YOU GOING?
I CAN'T STARE AT GRAPHS. I HAVE OTHER THINGS TO FIGURE OUT.

ALEA...
JANN, SOMETHING HAPPEN?
IT'S OKAY, DENIS. WE'RE GOING FOR A WALK.

WHEN WE CAME BACK FROM THE LAST EXPEDITION, YOU'D BEEN *FED* SOMETHING ABOUT DISCOVERY TEAM'S WORTH.
STEVEN TOLD YOU THAT, DIDN'T HE?

"THEY ENDANGER EVERYONE. THEY DON'T FOCUS ON IMMEDIATE SURVIVAL NEEDS". SOUND ABOUT RIGHT?
THOSE PEOPLE--AND THERE ARE A LOT OF THEM--THEY'RE *SCARED*. THEY'VE GIVEN UP HOPE.

BUT HE WASN'T LIKE THAT. HE DIDN'T GIVE UP.

BUT HE DID, ALEA. HE DID.
YOU DON'T WANT TO SEE IT THAT WAY. I DON'T BLAME YOU.

HE WAS PLANNING TO BE AN ENGINEER.

MY BABY GIRL.

OKAY, HERE'S WHAT'S UP.
THE CELL'S PASSED, BUT WHAT IT LEFT BEHIND IS STILL A VERY REAL PROBLEM.
WHERE WE SEE BLUE SKY AND PRETTY CLOUDS, IN REALITY THERE'S A MOUNTAIN OF ICE.
THAT MEANS PLANNING TEAM NEEDS US.
THEY NEED YOUR CLEVER BRAIN.

BUT YOU'RE NOT READY.
MOM, IT'S NOT MY FAULT--
THAT WASN'T A JUDGMENT. IT'S HOW IT IS.

I KNOW I COULD MAKE YOU GO BACK IN THERE TO DO YOUR JOB AND YOU'D LISTEN.
YOU'D TRY.
BUT THE OUTPOST NEEDS YOUR UNDIVIDED ATTENTION--AND THEY'RE NOT GOING TO GET IT.

SO, WHATEVER YOU WERE GOING TO RUN OFF AND DO--WHATEVER YOU THINK WILL GET YOU READY--
--DO EXACTLY THAT, FOR EXACTLY AS LONG AS IT TAKES.

THEN COME BACK HERE AND SHOW THE SCARED AND THE HOPELESS HOW WRONG THEY ARE.
SOUND GOOD?

I WAS SO BAD AT THE RACES. I HAD THE BREATH AND THE STRENGTH, BUT NO COORDINATION. NOT ANY OF IT.
I KNOCKED A TOOTH OUT ONE TIME. JUST SMACKED MY FACE RIGHT INTO THE GROUND.
I'M SITTING THERE BAWLING, HANDS OVER MY MOUTH--AND EVERYONE'S PASSING ME BY BECAUSE THEY DON'T WANT TO FINISH LAST.
MAYBE YOU WERE ONE OF THEM.
ANYWAY, THIS ONE BOY STOPS. HE ASKS TO SEE MY MOUTH, TAKES THIS LONG LOOK...
...AND THEN HE STARTS LAUGHING. LAUGHING AND LAUGHING.
AND HE SAYS, LIKE, "IF I GIVE YOU A HEAD START, WILL YOU STOP CRYING?"
AND I TELL HIM I WILL JUST BECAUSE I WANT THE HEAD START. I WANT THE CHANCE.
AND HE HELPS ME UP. AND I GET THE HEAD START.
AND THEN I TIE FOR LAST WITH MY NEW FRIEND.
THAT WAS STEVEN.

HOW ARE YOU NOT BAWLING RIGHT NOW AFTER SHARING THAT?
GOOD TIMES ARE GOOD TIMES. IT FEELS NICE TO THINK ABOUT THEM.
EVEN MY SINGULARITY. IT WON'T HAPPEN FOR TWELVE MORE DAYS, BUT I SMILE WHENEVER I IMAGINE IT.
I THINK OF ANYTHING HAPPY AND IT JUST REMINDS ME HOW WRONG IT IS THAT HE'S GONE.
IT'S A TRAGEDY, LYSS, AND WE HAVE NO IDEA WHY IT HAPPENED. HOW CAN EVERYONE IGNORE THAT?
CAN'T REALLY IGNORE THE UNKNOWN. IT'S EVERYWHERE, ALL THE TIME.
ALL I KNOW IS, WHAT HAPPENED TO STEVEN, IT HAPPENED. THERE'S NO CHANGING IT.
JUST LIKE NO ONE CAN TAKE AWAY THE DAY STEVEN AND I MET.
I KNOW WHICH ONE I'D RATHER THINK ABOUT.

INTERNSHIP'S ON HOLD, I SEE.
MITCHELL.
WHAT I DID AT THE SERVICE...
YOU WERE UPSET. WE ALL WERE.
I'VE BEEN THINKING ABOUT WHAT YOU SAID. STEVEN DIDN'T MOPE. HE WASN'T ONE OF THOSE LOSERS WHO CAN'T HACK IT.
BUT IT'S NOT LIKE HE LEFT A NOTE. WE'LL NEVER KNOW WHAT LED HIM TO--
WHAT I'M SAYING IS, HE WASN'T SPINELESS...
BUT HE STARTED HANGING OUT WITH SOMEONE WHO IS, DIDN'T HE?

WHERE'D ALEA GO?
SHE'S TAKING CARE OF SOMETHING.

HE APPRECIATED THE HELP YOU GAVE HIM.
HE, UH, HE WANTED TO MAKE HIS DAD PROUD.
YEAH. HE DID. DEFINITELY.

YOUR MOM'S GOTTA BE RUNNING IN CIRCLES OVER THIS, HUH?
SHE'S NOT--

I DON'T CALL HER THAT. I MEAN, IT'S NOT...
I CALL HER KAREN. EXCEPT AT WORK, THEN IT'S CHIEF.
IT'S NOT IMPORTANT.
SO, YOUR MOM, THE CHIEF...

DID SHE FIGURE OUT THE WHOLE DEAL WITH THE *AIRLOCK?*

AIRLOCK? HOW DO YOU MEAN?
WELL, WE BOTH KNOW HE DIDN'T GUESS THE CODE, RIGHT?

HE DIDN'T SEEM OFF TO YOU, DID HE? SAD?
HE...NO, HE WAS... I THOUGHT HE WAS FINE.
SCRATCH SCRATCH
GOTTA BE SOMETHING...

WHAT DID HE SAY THE LAST TIME YOU SAW HIM?
HOW--?
HOW DO YOU KNOW ABOUT THAT?

WHAT?
I SAW YOU, SAM. I WAS--
YOU SAW--?

YOU CAN'T--
DON'T TELL ANYONE I WAS IN THE AIRLOCK.
PLEASE.

THAT YOU--? YOU WERE IN THE AIRLOCK?
SHH.
WITH STEVEN?
SHH, DON'T.

THAT'S WHAT YOU SAID, SAM!
I DIDN'T.
I--

SAM?!

WHAT JUST HAPPENED? WHAT DID HE DO?
WANT ME TO GET HIM?

ALEA--
NO.
HE KNOWS SOMETHING.

AND I'M GETTING IT OUT OF HIM.

WHAT?
ARE WE REALLY DOING THIS AGAIN?
NO, SAM. WE'RE GOING TO DO SOMETHING A LITTLE DIFFERENT THIS TIME.

BECAUSE I HAVE STEVEN'S PARENTS, I HAVE COUNCIL MEMBERS, DESPERATE FOR AN EXPLANATION I DON'T HAVE.
BECAUSE EVERY DAY, THEY ONLY GET MORE INSISTENT.

SO YOU WILL HELP ME ASSURE THEM THE AIRLOCK IS SECURE, THAT THIS WON'T HAPPEN AGAIN.
IS ANY OF THIS GETTING THROUGH TO YOU? DO YOU HAVE NO COMPASSION?

SAM--
I'LL TELL YOU HOW I GOT THE CODE.
AND?

AND THAT'S IT. THAT PLUGS THE LEAK AND GETS EVERYONE OUT OF YOUR HAIR.
THE REST IS IRRELEVANT.

DO YOU THINK SUSPENDING YOUR INTERNSHIP IS THE WORST I CAN DO?
OR DO YOU JUST NOT RESPECT ME?

MAYBE YOU DON'T SEE IT, BUT I'M--
I NEVER ONCE PULLED "WHAT WOULD YOUR PARENTS THINK?" OR ANY OF THAT, HAVE I?
YOU KIND OF ARE NOW, SAYING THAT.

WE'RE STILL UNDER EMERGENCY PROTOCOLS.
THERE'S A MASSIVE BLOCK OF DEADLY ICE OVER OUR HEADS--I DON'T NEED YOUR SHIT ON TOP OF IT!

IF YOU DON'T TELL ME EVERYTHING, YOU'RE DONE ON SECURITY TEAM.
DONE.

DO YOU WANT ME TO TELL YOU HOW I GOT THE CODE?
OR DO YOU WANT ME TO TELL YOU NOTHING?

DAMN IT, SAM.
HOW'D YOU GET SO GOOD AT THIS?

HE'S NEVER WITH ANYBODY, NEVER TALKS TO ANYBODY--
--HE DOES TALK TO HIMSELF SOMETIMES, BUT IT'S ALMOST MUMBLING SO I CAN'T MAKE IT OUT--
--BUT, LIKE, THERE'S NOTHING HE CHERISHES, NO PERSON OR THING TO USE AS LEVERAGE.

HE DOESN'T EVEN SEEM TO BE INTERNING FOR SECURITY TEAM ANYMORE.

PLIP!

I DON'T KNOW HOW TO GET TO HIM.
COULD YOU PLEASE, MAYBE, TRY NOT MANIPULATING ANOTHER PERSON?
SNEAKING AROUND, INVADING PRIVACY?
LYSS, IT'S--
I MEAN, WHAT ELSE AM I SUPPOSED TO DO?

HE KNOWS WHY STEVEN WAS IN THE AIRLOCK. HE WAS THERE, BUT SINCE I FOUND OUT--
IF HE GETS JUST A GLIMPSE OF ME, HE WALKS AWAY. EVERY TIME.

HE DOESN'T EVEN GO TO LUNCH ANYMORE.
CLOSEST I'VE EVEN COME TO COMMUNICATING WITH HIM...

...IS THIS.

What I said was a mistake. Please don't tell anyone.
It could get people in serious trouble.

"SERIOUS TROUBLE?"
HE DOESN'T KNOW WHAT TROUBLE IS, BUT I'D BE HAPPY TO SHOW HIM...
MITCHELL...

FINE.
THEN TELL EVERYONE HE WAS IN THE AIRLOCK. HE'LL HAVE TO CONFESS WHAT HE KNOWS.

WE DO THAT, SAM GETS IN TROUBLE.
ALL THE BETTER.
NO, BECAUSE IF HE GETS IN TROUBLE, WHAT DO WE FIND OUT?
NOTHING. THE COUNCIL WILL KEEP IT ALL UNDER WRAPS AND WE'LL NEVER KNOW WHAT HAPPENED TO STEVEN.

SO THAT'S WHY YOU NEED LEVERAGE. MAKES SENSE. STILL--
YOU DON'T NEED LEVERAGE, ALEA...

...YOU ALREADY HAVE IT.

THAT'S YOUR SOLUTION, JANN?
ALL THESE MINDS TOGETHER IN ONE PLACE, AND YOU GET "DIG OUR WAY OUT AND CARVE THE ICE WITH LASERS".
WE ANGLE THE TRENCHES RIGHT, THE SUN DOES THE REST FOR US. MELTING STARTS, EXPOSING THE DOME, WARMING THE OUTER SURFACE--
YOU DON'T HAVE THE EQUIPMENT. OR ENOUGH ENVIRO-SUITS.
WE'VE ALREADY PUT OUT FEELERS TO FABRICATION TEAM. WE HAVE POTENTIAL OVERTIME VOLUNTEERS.
THE WHOLE THING'S DOABLE WITHIN--
SO, YOU'RE ALREADY TELLING EVERYONE WE'RE GOING AHEAD WITH IT.
CHIEF...WE EXPLAINED IT ISN'T A SURE THING YET.
NO. IT MOST DEFINITELY ISN'T A SURE THING.
THE AIRLOCK IS OUR GREATEST SECURITY THREAT. EVERY TIME WE OPEN IT, WE PLACE EVERYONE AT RISK.
I GET YOUR HESITATION. JOSH AND NADINE DO, TOO.
YOUR RECENT SECURITY LAPSE HAS EVERYONE ON EDGE, BUT--
DIDN'T YOUR HUSBAND HAVE ANOTHER IDEA?

HEAT CONDUCTION THROUGH THE DOME, WASN'T IT? I'D RATHER BE WITHOUT OUR FAKE SKY THAN WITHOUT OUR REAL HOME.
HOW DID YOU--?
WITHOUT THAT SKY, WE'LL BE JUST AS DEAD-- ONLY IT'LL BE A LONG AND MISERABLE DEATH.
THAT'S DEBATABLE. BUT IT'S OBVIOUS CONDUCTION IS MUCH LESS RISKY. DON'T BE BLIND TO IT.
I'M NOT--
SURE, THERE'S LESS OF AN IMMEDIATE RISK, BUT IN THE LONG TERM...
YOU KNOW, MAYBE YOU'D BETTER APPRECIATE IT IF YOU HAD SOMETHING TO LOSE, LIKE A CHILD OF YOUR OWN.
SOMEONE'S MORE VESTED IN WHISPERING TO SECURITY TEAM THAN IN SAVING THE OUTPOST.
IT WASN'T ME, BUT, YOU KNOW, TEAMS ARE SUPPOSED TO BE TRANSPARENT...
WHEN IT MAKES SENSE TO BE, JOSH. AFTER A COURSE OF ACTION'S BEEN DECIDED ON.
JANN, PLANNING TEAM'S A COLLECTIVE. WE'RE IN THIS TOGETHER. THERE'S NO NEED--
GREAT, NADINE.
THEN, NEXT TIME IT'S YOUR TURN TO PITCH THE CHIEF.

IT'S BEEN SAID THAT OUR KIND ONCE HAD A LIFESPAN AS LONG AS ONE HUNDRED YEARS.
EVEN LONGER, THANKS TO ALL WE'D LEARNED.

IMAGINE-- SOMEONE THAT OLD TODAY MIGHT HAVE KNOWN OUR FOUNDERS. THINK OF ALL THEY COULD TELL US...
HOW WE MANAGED IN THOSE EARLY DAYS. HOW WE ADAPTED TO STAND IN THE FACE OF OUR FATE. WHAT THEY INTENDED FOR US.

THINK OF WHAT THEY WOULD MAKE OF WHAT WE'VE BECOME, AND OF WHAT OUR CHILDREN ARE TODAY.

SAW YOU STARING AT THE DOME.
WONDERING IF IT'LL COLLAPSE ON US?
NO...

...I'M THINKING ABOUT WHAT MIGHT KEEP THAT FROM HAPPENING.

STARTING TO WONDER IF YOU WERE GOING TO SHOW. I KNOW YOU GOT MY NOTE.
I'M... ONLY HERE TO CLARIFY.
WHEN I WROTE THERE'D BE TROUBLE, I DIDN'T MEAN JUST FOR ME AND THE CHIEF.
THERE'D BE AN INQUIRY. I'D HAVE TO TELL THEM HOW I GOT THE AIRLOCK CODE.
THEY'D DISCOVER I JACKED IT WHEN THE CHIEF USED IT TO LET YOUR PARENTS OUT.
MOST EVERYONE WANTS DISCOVERY TEAM TO GO AWAY. ALL THEY NEED IS AN EXCUSE.
YOU'D DO THAT TO US?
I WOULDN'T HAVE ANY OTHER CHOICE, WOULD I?

WAIT.
WHY WON'T YOU JUST--
PLEASE. DON'T YOU UNDERSTAND? I HAVE TO KNOW WHAT STEVEN DID, WHY HE--

I WON'T SAY ANYTHING--NOT TO MY PARENTS, NOT LYSS, MITCHELL...

I CAN'T.
I CAN'T DO THAT.

WHY NOT?

YOU NEED TO LET IT GO.

LET'S KEEP MOVING FORWARD. ASSUME THAT WHATEVER WE SAY HERE REACHES THE CHIEF.
WITH THAT IN MIND...

...WE EITHER NEED TO GO WITH THE BACKUP PLAN ***SHE*** LIKES, OR WE MAKE THE MOST ***SOUND*** PLAN HAPPEN BY GOING OVER HER HEAD.
I KNOW WHICH I CHOOSE.

YOU WANT TO GO TO THE COUNCIL? THEY DON'T LOVE US--BY WHICH I MEAN YOU AND ME.
WELL, THAT'S... ENTIRELY TRUE. WHO HERE HAS PULL WITH THE RIGHT PEOPLE?

I CAN PRESENT IT, BUT I CAN'T PROMISE ANYTHING. THEY'LL HEAR ME OUT, AT LEAST.
BUT THE CHIEF, SHE DOESN'T HAVE TO DO WHAT THE COUNCIL SAYS. SHE HAS THE LAST WORD ON SECURITY ISSUES.

WHEN THEY HEAR THAT IDIOT PLAN SHE WANTS TO PULL, WE'LL ***SEE*** WHO HAS FINAL SAY.
SORRY, DENIS.
IT'S A FAIR ANALYSIS.

MOM?
I'LL GO GET THE CONVERSATION STARTED. WISH ME LUCK.

YOU KNOW WHO SAM IS, RIGHT? THE CHIEF'S BOY?
OF COURSE. SHE TOOK HIM IN AFTER THE LAST CELL.
RIGHT. WELL, HE WAS INTERNING WITH SECURITY TEAM, BUT I THINK HE GOT SUSPENDED.
AND... WHAT'S THAT HAVE TO DO WITH ANYTHING?

HE...KINDA KEEPS TO HIMSELF. I THINK MAYBE SOMETHING'S WRONG.
YOU'RE WORRIED ABOUT HIM?

DO YOU THINK SHE'S PUNISHING HIM FOR SOMETHING OUT OF...
LOVE, OR...?
WHAT I MEAN IS, DO YOU THINK THE CHIEF WOULD DO ANYTHING FOR SAM? EVEN THOUGH HE ISN'T REALLY HERS?

WELL, I THINK--
SHE CARES ABOUT SAM, WANTS HIM TO SUCCEED, LOVES HIM LIKE HER OWN SON.
BUT WHEN A CHILD'S YOURS FROM THE START-- WHEN THEY COME FROM YOU...

...THERE'S A BOND YOU DON'T GET ANY OTHER WAY.
IT'S JUST THE WAY IT IS.

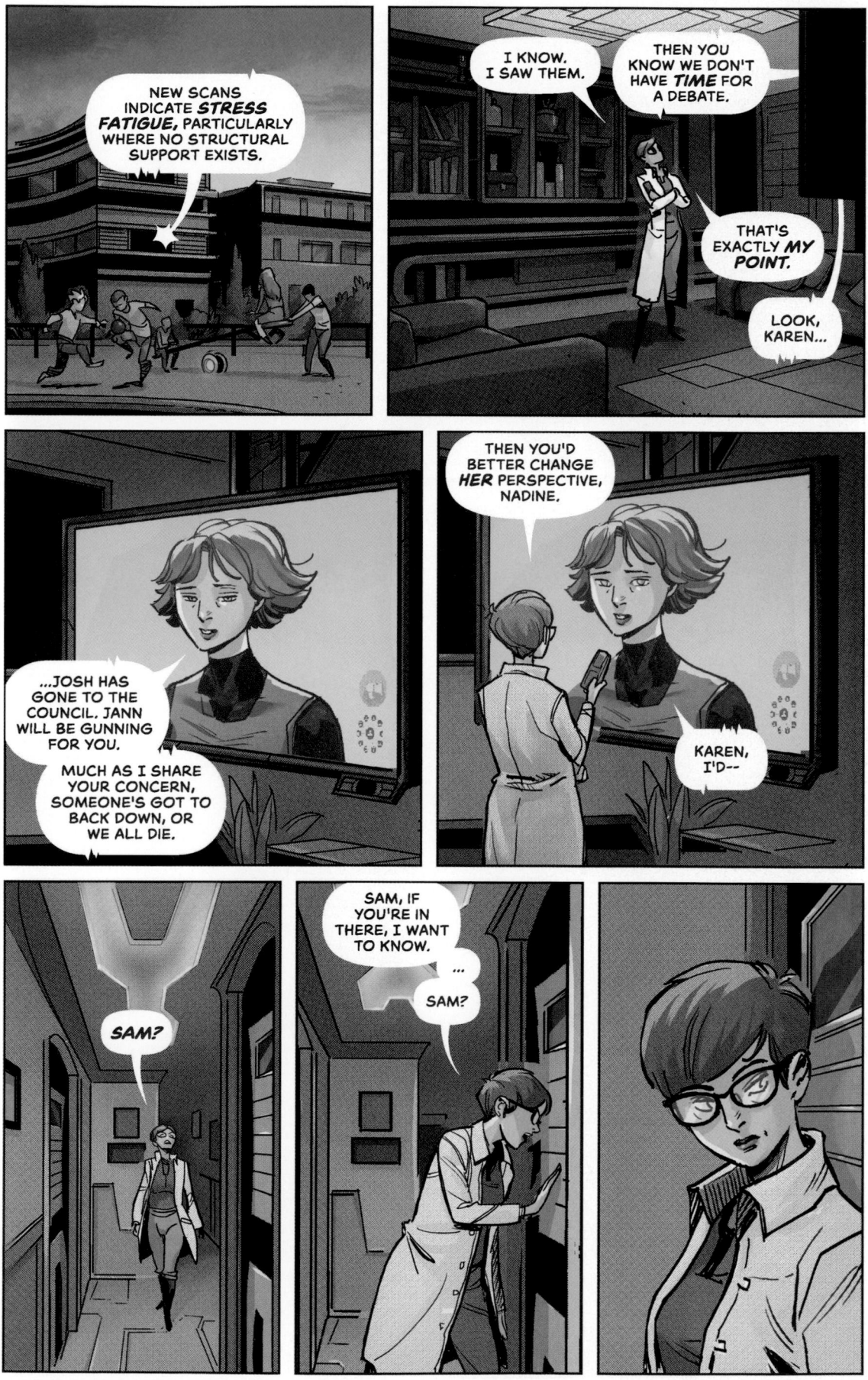
NEW SCANS INDICATE STRESS FATIGUE, PARTICULARLY WHERE NO STRUCTURAL SUPPORT EXISTS.
I KNOW. I SAW THEM.
THEN YOU KNOW WE DON'T HAVE TIME FOR A DEBATE.
THAT'S EXACTLY MY POINT.
LOOK, KAREN...
...JOSH HAS GONE TO THE COUNCIL. JANN WILL BE GUNNING FOR YOU.
MUCH AS I SHARE YOUR CONCERN, SOMEONE'S GOT TO BACK DOWN, OR WE ALL DIE.
THEN YOU'D BETTER CHANGE HER PERSPECTIVE, NADINE.
KAREN, I'D--
SAM?
SAM, IF YOU'RE IN THERE, I WANT TO KNOW.
...
SAM?

This is where we're going to...
I thought that I could make it without you...
BUT IT'S POINTLESS NOW, AS YOU CAN SEE...
WE MOVE TOGETHER IN THE STARRY...
--VISITOR.
YOU HAVE A VISITOR.
CAN WE TALK?

LET'S HEAR IT. WHAT DID YOUR MOTHER SEND YOU TO TELL ME?
SHE...
WHY WOULD SHE SEND ME?
THEN WHAT DO YOU WANT?

HAVE YOU FOUND ANYTHING OUT? ABOUT STEVEN?
ALEA, YOU CAN'T--

I KNOW YOU WERE CLOSE, BUT DO YOU THINK IT'S APPROPRIATE TO COME TO MY HOME AND ASK ME FOR A PROGRESS REPORT?
DO YOU THINK THAT'S *RESPECTFUL?*

DO *YOU* THINK IT'S RESPECTFUL TO KEEP EVERYONE IN THE DARK?

OKAY.
OKAY.
I'M NOT SURE HOW YOU THOUGHT THIS CONVERSATION WAS GOING TO GO, BUT NOW IT'S TIME FOR YOU TO--

I KNOW WHY YOU HAVE SAM ON SUSPENSION.

I KNOW ABOUT THE AIRLOCK.
WHAT ABOUT THE AIRLOCK?

STEVEN. AND SAM.

WHATEVER YOU THINK YOU HEARD, YOU SHOULD BE CAREFUL.
RUMORS ARE DANGEROUS.

YOU'RE RIGHT. THEY ARE.
THEY REALLY ARE.

THE THING ABOUT RUMORS, ANYONE CAN START ONE.
AND ANOTHER THING IS THAT SOMETIMES THEY TURN OUT TO BE TRUE.

LIKE, IF ONE WAS STARTED ABOUT HOW SAM OPENED THE DOOR.

DO THAT, AND I'LL PRESENT EVIDENCE YOUR FRIEND MANIPULATED MY SON INTO UNWITTINGLY ASSISTING HIS SUICIDE.
THAT ISN'T TRUE!
HIS COWARDLY SUICIDE.

I DON'T CARE WHO YOUR PARENTS ARE. THREATEN ME AND MINE AGAIN, AND THERE WILL BE A COST.
DO YOU UNDERSTAND ME?

SHIT...
SHIT...
MISCALCULATED.
AGAIN.
THANKS, MOM...

OOH, SAM, YOU'RE IN TROUBLE NOW, I BET...

SHE'S GOING AFTER SAM...

NO ONE'S *HOME.*

WHAT THE SHIT ARE *YOU?*

I CHANGED THE CODE.
HOPED MAYBE I WAS LOCKING YOU IN.

SAM, WHAT ARE YOU EVEN THINKING?!
WHAT?
DON'T "WHAT" ME.

ALEA.
SHE KNOWS YOU WERE IN THE AIRLOCK WITH STEVEN. SHE KNOWS YOU WITNESSED WHAT HE--
AND I KNOW SHE KNOWS BECAUSE SHE JUST THREW IT IN MY FACE!

SHE DOESN'T--
I TRIPPED UP, SAID THE WRONG THING. SHE CAN'T PROVE ANY OF IT, THERE'S NO WAY--

THINK IT MATTERS IF SHE HAS PROOF? IF THIS GETS AROUND--IF THE COUNCIL HEARS? HER PARENTS?
THAT'S IT, SAM. I WON'T BE ABLE TO PROTECT YOU FROM WHAT COMES NEXT.
IT DOESN'T MATTER IF YOU'RE MY SON.

IT'S OKAY.
IT IS.
I MADE IT SO SHE WON'T TELL ANYONE.
YOU HAVE TO TRUST ME.

YOU KNOW THAT'S NOT ENOUGH...

PLEASE. IT'S MY MESS. I CAN HANDLE IT.
LET ME SHOW YOU I CAN.

NO. I CAN'T BE IN THE DARK ON THIS, SAM. IT'S TOO SERIOUS.

I KNOW HOW BAD IT SEEMS. I PROMISE, THOUGH, I'LL MAKE YOU PROUD.
LET ME.

SOON ENOUGH, I WON'T HAVE TO CARE WHAT THEY THINK. EVER.
JUST ONE FAVOR BEFORE I GO, OKAY?
THIS NEW WORLD YOU GET TO MAKE-- MORE THAN ANYTHING, I HOPE YOU CH-CH-
CH-
CH-
CH-
CH-
CH-
UNEXPECTED END OF ARCHIVE. MEDIA NOT FOUND.
WOULD YOU LIKE TO REPLAY THE AVAILABLE PORTION?
YES.
STAY HOME. YOU DON'T GO ANYWHERE.

WHERE ARE *YOU* GOING?
BACK TO WORK.
NOT-- NOT TO ALEA'S...

I SAID I'D GIVE YOU A SHOT.
I MEANT IT.
BUT THE FIRST SECOND YOU FEEL IT'S OUT OF YOUR HANDS-- THE *FIRST SECOND*--
I HEARD YOU. JUST... MAKING SURE.

NO.
NO.

I HAVE IT.
NOT TELLING YET.
TALK SOON.
NO.
NO.
NO.

TICK TICK TICK
ICK
TICK
WE'RE ALL ON EDGE.
IT'S GOOD TO BE ON EDGE. GOOD TO REMEMBER HOW IMPORTANT THIS IS.
DEATH ALWAYS HANGS OVER US. YOU'RE PLANNING TEAM, I'M NOT TELLING YOU ANYTHING NEW.
BUT IT'S NEVER BEEN THIS LITERAL. THAT MOUNTAIN OF ICE IS PRESSING DOWN ON US AS WE SPEAK.
WE HAVE TO GET OUT THERE AND DEAL WITH IT OUR WAY, OR ELSE WE WILL DIE.
THE COUNCIL WILL HAVE A LOT OF QUESTIONS ABOUT OUR PLAN.
WE NEED TO BE READY.
THE CHIEF DOESN'T LIKE THIS PLAN, AND SHE HAS MORE SWAY THAN ALL OF US COMBINED.
I PROMISE YOU, SHE'LL BE VIGILANT.
AND BY VIGILANT, I MEAN RUTHLESS.

210079034 1
I WANT TO SEE INSIDE THERE.
IT'S RESTRICTED ACCESS, ALEA.
OH, BUT YOU'RE ALLOWED?
YOU KEEP IGNORING ME LIKE I HAVE NO RIGHT TO KNOW ANYTHING, AND I'M GETTING PRETTY TIRED--
PEOPLE LIKE YOU, LIKE MITCHELL--YOU PLOW INTO OTHER PEOPLE'S LIVES.
YOU DON'T THINK ABOUT ANYONE ELSE. YOU JUST DO IT.
YOU HAD NO RIGHT TO BE IN MY HOME, IN MY ROOM. YOU TOOK SOMETHING FROM ME.
YOUR MACHINE--
SAM, YOU CAN'T--
IT'S BIGGER THAN YOU OR ME. IT DOESN'T BELONG HIDDEN IN YOUR BEDROOM.

I COULD ONLY GET IT TO PLAY PART OF ONE RECORDING.
IT'S ALL THAT'S CACHED IN MEMORY. THE REST IS LOST, DOWN IN THE STEM.

SAM...I DON'T THINK ANYONE KNOWS THIS KIND OF THING EVEN EXISTS.
IT'S INFORMATION, PERSPECTIVE. A DOORWAY INTO OUR PAST. WE HAVE TO OPEN IT.

THIS ISN'T SOMETHING TAKEN FROM US IN THE CRASH LIKE EVERYTHING ELSE. I TRIED TO CONNECT. THE NETWORK WAS SEVERED.
SABOTAGED. DELIBERATELY.

THEY WANTED THE GENSHIP ANCESTRY PROJECT TO BE FORGOTTEN. ALL OUR HISTORY, WHERE WE COME FROM, WHAT WE WERE LIKE.
WHO WOULD WANT THAT?
MAYBE SOMEONE WHO HAS THEIR OWN IDEAS ABOUT WHAT WE OUGHTA BE.

THERE HAVE TO BE OTHERS WHO KNOW THE G.A.P. EXISTS. I THINK THEY'D RATHER KEEP IT FORGOTTEN.
IT'S SAFER IF NO ONE ELSE FINDS OUT WHAT WE KNOW.

SURE IS CONVENIENT HOW ALL YOUR SECRETS HAVE TO STAY SECRET.
YOU PROBABLY EVEN HAVE SOME EXCUSE WHY I CAN'T KNOW WHAT'S IN THAT PLACE.

BUNCH OF SCRAP. ELECTRICAL STUFF, PARTS, METAL.
AND CATS. THEY COME AND GO--THROUGH THE VENTS, I THINK. I WAS FEEDING THEM AS PART OF MY INTERNSHIP.

I ALWAYS WONDERED HOW THEY ALL KEPT--
HEY.
YOU'RE ACTUALLY TELLING ME THINGS.

THE WAREHOUSE IS PUBLIC KNOWLEDGE.
AND THE G.A.P., I MEAN...YOU'VE SEEN THE PROJECTOR. I'M NOT GONNA LIE ABOUT IT.

THEN WHY CAN'T YOU TELL ME ABOUT STEVEN?

YOU WANT THE PROJECTOR BACK, SAM?
THAT'S THE PRICE.

GET HIM!
SO DID YOU--
AHK!
--PUT HIM IN HIS PLACE OR WHAT?
DON'T WORRY ABOUT IT.
LYSS! THAT WAY!
IT'S NOT LIKE YOU NEED TO BEND HIM TO YOUR WILL ANYWAY, RIGHT?
ALL YOU NEED'S A FOOT IN THE DOOR AND THE REST'LL HAPPEN.
NO, GOT TO PUSH HIM SO HE UNDERS--
AHH!

NICE SHOT.
YOU WEREN'T FOCUSING.
IT'S NOT THE SAME WITHOUT FOUR PLAYERS, IS IT?
MADDIE COULD JOIN US.
YEAH, THAT'S NOT HAPPENING.
I SHOULDN'T BE DOING THIS IN THE FIRST PLACE.
HAVE TO STAY DISCIPLINED FOR MY DEBUT.
THAT'S RIGHT! NOT LONG AFTER MY SINGULARITY! SO EXCITING...
LOOK AT US. GUESS LIFE DOES GO ON.
IT'S A NICE DAY.
STEVEN WOULD'VE LIKED TODAY.

GOOD TO SEE THAT IN SPITE OF EVERYTHING, SHE HASN'T FORGOTTEN HOW TO HAVE FUN.

DON'T ENCOURAGE THAT, DAD. THEY'RE MAKING A HALF-NAKED PUBLIC SPECTACLE OF THEMSELVES.

WHAT'S THE POINT OF MAKING A SPECTACLE IF IT'S NOT IN PUBLIC?
ARE YOU *KIDDING* ME?
WHICH ANSWER WILL MAKE ACTUAL STEAM COME OUT OF YOUR EARS?

MOM-- DAD'S MAKING DUMB JOKES AGAIN.
I'LL LET THE COUNCIL KNOW, ELLA. HE'LL PAY FOR HIS CRIMES.
YES, GO AHEAD.

1:01:01
sunday
november
16
JANN.
HOPING YOU COULD SPARE A FEW MINUTES.

WHAT'S THIS ABOUT, KAREN?
YOUR DAUGHTER...

WHAT ABOUT MY DAUGHTER?
UH. THIS MIGHT SOUND--

BUT, UH...
DO YOU TRUST HER?

THE POINT OF THAT KIND OF QUESTION HAD BETTER MAKE ITSELF KNOWN BEFORE--

IT'S OKAY. I DON'T--
JUST...
YOU GIVE HER SPACE. YOU WANT HER TO LEARN FROM EXPERIENCE, YOU HOPE SHE'LL MAKE THE RIGHT CHOICES...

...BUT THERE'S A LINE, RIGHT? THERE'S A POINT WHERE YOU HAVE TO STEP IN, TAKE CONTROL.

OH. YOU'RE ASKING...
WELL...THE BEST I CAN SAY IS, WE HAVE TO TRUST OUR CHILDREN UNTIL THEY DO SOMETHING TO BREAK THAT TRUST.

AND WHEN THEY GO TOO FAR, THERE HAS TO BE SOME SORT OF CONSEQUENCE.

IS...SAM ALRIGHT, OR...?
HOW LONG WOULD IT TAKE TO GET ALL THE EQUIPMENT YOU NEED TO CUT INTO THE MOUNTAIN?

UH, TWENTY DAYS--ESTIMATED. BUT DENIS AND I CAN START CARVING A TUNNEL IMMEDIATELY.

ONCE YOU'RE CLEAR OF THE AIRLOCK DOOR, KEEPING IT ***CLOSED*** AS MUCH AS POSSIBLE IS YOUR TOP PRIORITY.
I'LL GET THINGS IN MOTION ON MY END.
YOU WILL?

JANN...
GOING OVER MY HEAD TO THE COUNCIL WOULD NEVER HAVE WORKED.
BUT I GET WHY YOU WANTED TO.

YOU NEED SLEEP.
MY PROJECTOR. YOU DIDN'T BRING IT.
I GET WHAT I WANT FIRST. THAT'S HOW THIS WORKS.
IF WE DO THIS, YOU DON'T SHARE ANY OF IT WITH ANYONE.
DONE.
AND I CAN'T TELL YOU WHY. WHY HE DID IT.
NO. NO, I WON'T AGREE TO THAT.
I MEAN IT. IF I KNEW, I'D TELL YOU.
PLEASE.

OKAY.
HE SAYS HE WANTS TO GO INTO THE AIRLOCK, AND YOU DON'T ASK HIM WHY?
OR, YOU DO ASK, AND HE DOESN'T SAY BUT YOU GO AHEAD WITH IT...?
IT'S NOT...
I WAS ALREADY THERE. HE CAME IN AFTER ME AND--
WHAT WERE YOU DOING IN THE AIRLOCK?
SAM?
SAM.
I REMEMBER THINKING, "STEVEN DIDN'T JUST PRIME THE OUTER DOOR TO OPEN, DID HE? WHY WOULD HE DO THAT?"
WHY WOULD HE DO THAT?
IT WAS COLD. SO COLD. THE WIND...
I COULD HARDLY TAKE IT.
HE STOOD RIGHT OUTSIDE THE DOOR UNTIL IT CLOSED. WAS HARD TO SEE, BUT...

...HE SMILED.

HE DIDN'T SAY ANYTHING TO YOU? AT ALL?
YOU'LL THINK I MADE IT UP.
TELL ME THE TRUTH. I DESERVE THE TRUTH.

IT'S... BIZARRE, STUPID.
SOUNDS LIKE, LIKE, LIKE A STORYTIME THING.
HE SAID--

IT'S UP TO YOU TO SAVE THEM, SAM.
YOU AND ALEA.

FOLLOW IT DOWN.

FOLLOW IT DOWN.

I KNOW HOW TENSE YOU ALL MUST FEEL.
I ALSO KNOW THIS ANNOUNCEMENT TOOK LONGER TO GET TO THAN ANY OF YOU WOULD HAVE LIKED.
WE HAD TO WEIGH ALL THE OPTIONS. WE HAD TO BE SURE.
TODAY, IN PARTNERSHIP WITH SECURITY TEAM AND THE COUNCIL, PLANNING TEAM IS LAUNCHING A ***PROACTIVE EMERGENCY INITIATIVE.***
THEIR OBJECTIVE WILL BE TO REMOVE THE DEADLY MOUNTAIN OF ICE OVER OUR HEADS.
MANY OF YOU ARE ASSISTING THE EFFORT, WHETHER BY PROVIDING EQUIPMENT OR BRAVING OUT INTO THE FROST.
THE REST OF YOU MAY HELP AS WELL. BY GOING ABOUT YOUR LIVES AND MAINTAINING DAY-TO-DAY OPERATIONS, YOU'RE KEEPING THE OUTPOST INTACT.
YOU PROVIDE THE VITAL REMINDER THAT, IF WE'RE TO SURVIVE HERE, OUR LIVES MUST GO ON UNIMPEDED.

HESITANT AS I AM TO STRESS THIS, OUR SUCCESS IS FAR FROM GUARANTEED. SOME FACTORS REMAIN OUT OF OUR CONTROL.
AND WE WILL BE USING THE AIRLOCK ON MULTIPLE OCCASIONS.
EVERY TIME WE OPEN THE AIRLOCK, WE EXPOSE THE OUTPOST TO THE POTENTIAL OF A BREACH.
AND ANY BREACH, NO MATTER HOW SMALL, COULD BE DISASTROUS FOR US.
OUR BEST AND BRIGHTEST ARE DOING ALL THEY CAN TO ENSURE THIS DOESN'T HAPPEN.
FOR MORE THAN TWO CENTURIES, AGAINST GREAT ODDS, WE'VE SURVIVED ON THIS WORLD.
I SAY TO YOU NOW, WITH FULL CONFIDENCE...
...WE WILL MAKE IT THROUGH THIS, TOO.

to be
continued

i wish i could
be there.
wish i could
see all the
incredible,
alien things.